Caterina Hughes
Illustrations by Abbie Cleave

The Very Special Dolphin

Bumblebee Books
London

BUMBLEBEE PAPERBACK EDITION

A CIP catalogue record for this title is
available from the British Library.

ISBN: 978-1-83934-057-4

Bumblebee Books is an imprint of
Olympia Publishers.

First Published in 2021

Bumblebee Books
Tallis House
2 Tallis Street
London
EC4Y 0AB

Printed in Great Britain

www.olympiapublishers.com

Dedication

For my son, I hope you realise how special you are.

THIS BOOK BELONGS TO:

_____

There was once a special little dolphin called Ralphie. Ralphie was unique.
He was orange with black stripes, he was kind, just like a dolphin,
and brave, just like a tiger.

Ralphie was different to the other dolphins, Ralphie was rare, Ralphie was special. His mummy was a dolphin, but his daddy was a tiger.

Although they both loved Ralphie very much, they could not live together.
Ralphie's mummy needed to live in the sea and
his daddy needed to live on the land.

Ralphie often felt sad and confused,
he wished he could live with his mummy and daddy together.

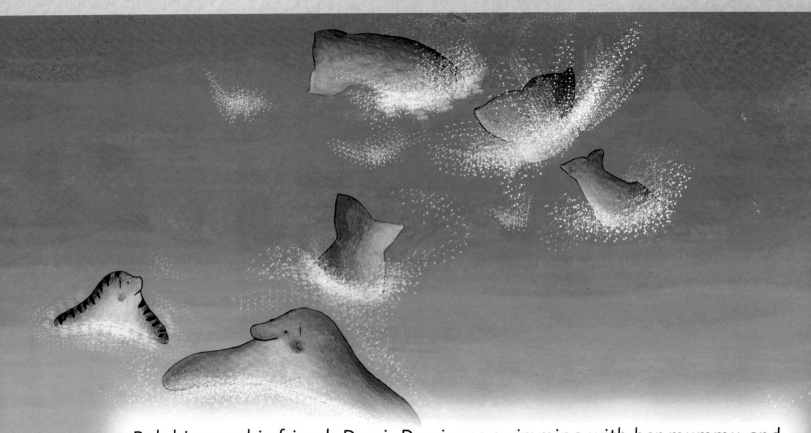

Ralphie saw his friend, Demi. Demi was swimming with her mummy and daddy. Ralphie wished that his daddy could live in the sea too.

Later that day, Ralphie saw Demi playing catch with her mummy and daddy.
"Why can't I play with my mummy and daddy like Demi?" Ralphie asked.
"Because you're special, darling," Ralphie's mummy replied.
But I don't want to be special, thought Ralphie.

Next, Ralphie saw Demi eating dinner with her mummy and daddy.
"Why can't I eat dinner with my mummy and daddy?" Ralphie asked.
"Because you're special, darling," Ralphie's mummy replied.
But I don't want to be special, thought Ralphie.

After dinner, Ralphie saw Demi's mummy and daddy put her to bed. "Why can't my mummy and daddy put me to bed?" Ralphie asked.

"Because you're special, darling," Ralphie's mummy replied.
But I don't want to be special, thought Ralphie as he drifted off to sleep.

The next day, when Ralphie woke up,
he went to spend the day on the land, with his daddy.

Ralphie played in the jungle with his daddy.
Ralphie heard the chirping, humming and buzzing sounds of the jungle.
"Why can't mummy and daddy play with me together?" Ralphie asked.
"Because you're special, darling," Ralphie's daddy replied.
But I don't want to be special, thought Ralphie.

Later, Ralphie ate dinner with his daddy in the jungle.
Ralphie tasted the sweet, delicious, tropical fruits of the jungle.
"Why can't I eat dinner with my mummy and daddy?" Ralphie asked.
"Because you're special, darling," Ralphie's daddy replied.
But I don't want to be special, thought Ralphie.

After dinner Ralphie's daddy put him to bed.
Ralphie lay under the roof of luscious green leaves.
"Why can't my mummy and daddy put me to bed?" Ralphie asked.
"Because you're special, darling," Ralphie's daddy replied.
But I don't want to be special, thought Ralphie as he drifted off to sleep.

The next day Ralphie went swimming in the sea with his mummy.
They saw Demi with her dad. Demi swam up to Ralphie.
"Where were you yesterday Ralphie? I didn't see you all day."
"I was exploring the land with my daddy."
The land? thought Demi, *but Ralphie is a Dolphin.*

Demi was so confused she thought long and
hard about all the things Ralphie could do on the land.
"Dad, can I go and explore the land like Ralphie?" asked Demi.
"No, darling, dolphins can't survive on land," Demi's dad replied.
"But, that's not fair, how come Ralphie explored the land?" Demi persisted.

"BECAUSE I AM SPECIAL," Ralphie smiled.

About the Author

My name is Caterina Hughes and I am a primary school teacher, I have written this book to help children with separated parents. I hope you like it as much as I do.